Learning to Read and Write
Step by Step!

Ready to Read and Write Preschool–Kindergarten
• big type and easy words
• picture clues
• drawing and first writing activities

For children who like to "tell" stories by drawing pictures and are eager to write.

Reading and Writing with Help Preschool–Grade 1
• basic vocabulary
• short sentences
• simple writing activities

For children who use letters, words, and pictures to tell stories.

Reading and Writing on Your Own Grades 1–3
• popular topics
• easy-to-follow plots
• creative writing activities

For children who are comfortable writing simple sentences on their own.

STEP INTO READING® Write-In Readers are designed to give every child a successful reading and writing experience. The grade levels are only guides. Children can progress through the steps at their own speed, developing confidence in their abilities, no matter what grade.

Remember, a lifetime love of reading and writing starts with a single step!

To Heidi Kilgras,
editor extraordinaire
—D.H.

To Elisa, Sosha's fabulous K-1 teacher
—S.W.

www.stepintoreading.com

Educators and librarians, for a variety of teaching tools, visit us at www.randomhouse.com/teachers

Library of Congress Control Number: 2003114931
ISBN 0-375-82893-1

Printed in the United States of America 10 9 8 7 6 5 4 3 2 1

STEP INTO READING, RANDOM HOUSE, and the Random House colophon are registered trademarks of Random House, Inc.

STEP INTO READING®

STEP 3

LITTLE WITCH LOVES TO WRITE

A Write-In Reader

by Deborah Hautzig and

_____

your name

illustrated by Sylvie Wickstrom and

_____

your name

Random House 🏠 New York

Little Witch was so sad!

She wanted to go

to summer camp again.

But Mother Witch said,

"No camp! We are going to visit

Aunt Sand Witch at the beach!"

Little Witch had never been

to the beach.

"I won't have anyone
to play with!" she cried.
Mother Witch smiled and said,
"I love it when you complain!"

5

Mother Witch packed a suitcase
full of witchy things.

Help Little Witch pack her suitcase.

Make a list of things

to bring to the beach:

The witches all got
on their broomsticks.
WHOOSH! They were off.
"I see Aunt Sand Witch's house!"
screamed Mother Witch.

The witches swooped down
and landed with a THUD.
"Welcome!" said Aunt Sand Witch.
"Welcome? Yuck!" said Aunt Nasty.
"Yeah, fine, hello,"
grumbled Mother Witch.
Little Witch liked
Aunt Sand Witch right away.

"Come on, Little Witch,"
said Cousin Dippy.
"Let's go to the beach!"
Scrubby and Bow-Wow
came, too.
"Look at the waves!"
cried Little Witch.

Cousin Dippy waved
at the ocean.
"Hello! Hello! Oh, the water
is so friendly!" she said.

That night the witches

had fried garbage for dinner.

"I picked this garbage myself,"

said Aunt Sand Witch proudly.

"It was all over the beach!"

"Yum," said Little Witch politely.

"It's too clean,"

grumbled Aunt Grouchy.

"It's not burned enough!"

said Aunt Nasty.

"Just for that,

YOU make the dessert!"

said Mother Witch.

Help Aunt Nasty
and Aunt Grouchy
make a witchy cake.
What should they call it?

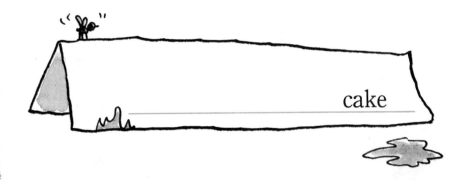

_____ cake

What should go in it?

Circle the ingredients.

MUD

Blood

SAW
DUST

Fish
Oil

Now draw the finished cake!

The next morning, Little Witch
put on her bathing suit and
went right to the beach.
There were <u>so</u> many people!
A girl and a boy
came over to her.
"Hi, I'm Rachel," said the girl.
"And this is Jonathan.
Are you on vacation, too?"
"Yes," said Little Witch shyly.

"You can help us build

a sand castle," said Jonathan.

"Oh, I LOVE helping!"

said Little Witch.

They made a castle with towers

and decorated it

with seashells and sticks.

They made up a story

about the prince and princess

who lived there.

What if you were a prince or a princess?
Finish this story about yourself
and your kingdom.

Once upon a time, there was a
prince named _____ and a
princess named _____ .
They lived in a _____ castle
on the island of _____ . One
day, they rode out to sea on their
pet _____ . There they met
_____ , the King of Dolphins.
He gave them each a _____ .
The most fun was when they

_____

The End!

Soon all the witches came
to the beach.
They sat under a giant
black umbrella.
"Yikes! Witches!" screamed Rachel.
"That's just my family,"
said Little Witch.
"I'm a witch, too."
"But there <u>are</u> no witches!"
said Jonathan.

"Yes, there are," said Little Witch.

"I will cast a spell to prove it!"

   "Beachy teachy,

   Sandy landy,

   Make these shells

   Turn into candy!"

POOF! The castle was now
decorated with lollipops,
jelly beans, and gummy worms.
"WOW!" said Rachel
and Jonathan.

Here's a spell for you
to finish!
Fill in the missing word:

Blowing, glowing,

Rainbow yum.

Now it's raining

Bubble _____!

Search for words you have seen
in this book.
Circle them.

```
b   u   b   b   l   e
e   g   l   o   w   f
a   u   o   y   u   m
n   m   w   j   z   a
s   p   e   l   l   q
d   w   i   t   c   h
```

Now finish the words you found:

___ e a n ___   b ___ o ___

b ___ b ___ ___ e   ___ u m

___ p ___ l l   ___ o y

g l ___ ___ ___   ___ ___ t c h

Little Witch ran to Mother Witch.

"I have two new friends!"

said Little Witch happily.

"You ALWAYS make friends,"

grumbled Mother Witch.

"It makes me sick!"

Little Witch told her new friends
about her best friend, Marcus.
Then she had an idea.
"Let's make a list of things
you find on a beach.
Then we can collect them
for Marcus!"

"It can be a Finders' Club!"

said Jonathan.

"Wait here," said Rachel.

"I will get paper and a pencil."

Little Witch stopped her.

"We don't need them!"

said Little Witch.

"I can write in the sand!"

Little Witch showed Jonathan

how to write words.

Give Little Witch a head start.
Make a list of things she can
collect for Marcus.

FINDERS' CLUB LIST

The list got longer and longer.

The Finders' Club

kept them very busy.

Rachel was a great finder.

Little Witch put all the things

they found for Marcus

in an old rubber boot.

The witches went

to the beach each day.

Cousin Dippy sat and waved.

Aunt Sand Witch and

Mother Witch swapped recipes.

Aunt Grouchy and Aunt Nasty

read books about curses.

"IT'S TOO HOT!"

screamed Aunt Nasty.

"I HATE IT HERE!"

growled Aunt Grouchy.

So Little Witch said,

"I will cast a cool-off spell!"

Little Witch said:

"Shivery slivery,
Eskimo,
Make it cool
With lots of snow!"

POOF! It began to snow—
but only on the witches.

"You are a really good witch,"
said Rachel and Jonathan.
"WE KNOW! SHE DRIVES US
CRAZY!" yelled Mother Witch.

Little Witch told the witches

about the Finders' Club

and how much she missed Marcus.

"So send him a postcard!"

said Aunt Sand Witch.

POOF! She handed Little Witch

a postcard with a seagull on it.

"Pretty!" said Little Witch.

"Pretty ugly!" said Aunt Grouchy.

Little Witch wrote:

Dear Marcus,
The beach is great!
I have two new friends
and a surprise for you.
I hope camp is fun!
Love,
    from Little Witch

for Marcus
_____
_____
_____

place
stamp
here

Instead of mailing the postcard,

she asked Scrubby to deliver it.

Marcus wrote a letter
to Little Witch from camp.
Pretend you are away at camp
and write a letter to Little Witch.

Dear Little Witch,

_____

_____

_____

_____

_____

_____

_____

Soon it was almost time

for the Witch family to go home.

Little Witch packed up

her Finders' Club collection.

"I don't WANT to leave!"

cried Little Witch.

"Hurray! You are complaining

again!" said Mother Witch.

Aunt Sand Witch hugged

Little Witch and said,

"Don't worry. You can come again!"

The witches had their
last dinner on the porch.
Aunt Sand Witch made
her famous
rotten-fish sandwiches.

Jonathan and Rachel

came to say goodbye.

"We will miss you!" they said.

"I will write to you

as soon as I learn how!"

said Jonathan.

"Remember what I showed you!"

said Little Witch.

Mother Witch glared
at Little Witch.
"You are being nice again.
What am I going to DO
with you?"
"That's YOUR problem!"
said Little Witch with a twinkle.